Look for these Just Right Books™

Just Right for 2's and 3's

MINE! A SESAME STREET BOOK ABOUT SHARING
By Linda Hayward
Illustrated by Norman Gorbaty

SALLY WANTS TO HELP
By Cindy Wheeler

Just Right for 3's and 4's

THE RUNAWAY CHRISTMAS TOY
By Linda Hayward
Illustrated by Ann Schweninger

SWEETIE AND PETIE
By Katharine Ross
Illustrated by Lisa McCue

Just Right for 4's and 5's

PATRICK AND TED RIDE THE TRAIN
By Geoffrey Hayes

THE CLEVER CARPENTER
By R. W. Alley

Library of Congress Cataloging-in-Publication Data:
Hayward, Linda. The runaway Christmas toy. (A Just right book) SUMMARY: When Santa makes a toy train with wheels that roll for a special little boy, the train tries to roll out of Santa's workshop. [1. Toys—Fiction.   2. Christmas—Fiction] I. Schweninger, Ann, ill. II. Title.   PZ7.H31495Ru 1988   [E]   88-4522   ISBN: 0-394-89693-9; 0-394-99693-3 (lib. bdg.)

Manufactured in the United States of America   1 2 3 4 5 6 7 8 9 0

JUST RIGHT BOOKS is a trademark of Random House, Inc.

A Just Right Book

The Runaway Christmas Toy

By Linda Hayward

Illustrated by Ann Schweninger

Random House 🏠 New York

Text copyright © 1988 by Random House, Inc. Illustrations copyright © 1988 by Ann Schweninger. All rights reserved under International and Pan-American Copyright Conventions. Published in the United States by Random House, Inc., New York, and simultaneously in Canada by Random House of Canada Limited, Toronto.

Once there was a boy who wanted a toy train for Christmas. It had to have a bell that went ding and it had to have wheels that really rolled.

He wrote a letter to Santa Claus and told him so!

As soon as Santa Claus read the letter, he
went into his workshop and made a toy train
with a bell that went ding and with wheels that
really rolled.

Then he put the toy train on a shelf.
"Wait here until Christmas Eve," said Santa
Claus. "Then I will take you to a wonderful
place—a boy's house!"

The toy train did not like staying in one place. It wanted to roll.

It rolled down to the end of the shelf. DİNG, DİNG! It rolled down to the other end. DİNG, DİNG!

But the toy train could not roll far. The shelf was just not big enough for a train with wheels that really rolled.

On Christmas Eve it was time to fill Santa's sack. Santa's elves took the toy train down from the shelf and set it on the floor with all of the other toys.

When the little toy train saw the great big floor, it started to roll.

"Stop, little train!" cried the elves, and they ran after it—Jingle, Jingle! But the toy train did not stop. It just kept rolling. DING, DING!

The little toy train rolled right past a stuffed lion with a yellow yarn mane and a floppy tail.

"Stop, little train!" cried the lion, and he flopped his tail—PHLOOP, PHLOOP!

Jingle, jingle, PHLOOP, PHLOOP—but the toy train did not stop. It just kept rolling. DING, DING!

It rolled right past a toy robot with flashing lights and a whirly head.

"Stop, little train!" cried the robot, and he flashed his lights—**BLEEP, BLEEP!**

Jingle, jingle, PHLOOP, PHLOOP, **BLEEP, BLEEP**— but the toy train did not stop. It just kept rolling. DING, DING!

It rolled right past a teddy bear with fuzzy brown paws and a toy drum.

"Stop, little train!" cried the bear, and he
beat his drum—**BRRRRUM, BRRRRUM!**
Jingle, jingle, PHLOOP, PHLOOP, **BLEEP, BLEEP,
BRRRRUM, BRRRRUM**—but the toy train did not
stop. It just kept rolling. DING, DING!

Suddenly it rolled right up to some big black
boots and came to a stop. D^INK! Santa Claus
leaned over and picked up the toy train.

"Look at this—a runaway Christmas toy!" said Santa. His eyes twinkled. "Don't you want to go with me to a boy's house tonight? A boy's house is big enough for a train with wheels that really roll."

That sounded wonderful to the little toy train. DĪNG, DĪNG!

Then Santa Claus put the toy train in his
sack with all of the other toys and drove away
in his sleigh.

When he came to the house of the boy who wanted a toy train for Christmas, Santa took the little train out of his sack and left it under the Christmas tree.

And on Christmas morning when the boy
woke up, he found it. *HOORAY!*